REGINA SHEN: SALVAGE

LANCE ERLICK

Finlee Augare Books (Chicago)

This is a work of fiction. All of the characters, organizations, and events portrayed herein are either products of the author's imagination or are used fictitiously, and any similarities to actual persons, organizations, or events is entirely coincidental. Also, though locations used in this work exist, for dramatic effect details have been altered. Accordingly, they should be considered fictitious.

Finlee Augare Books, Chicago, IL
ISBN: 978-1-943080-10-6 (print)
ISBN: 978-1-943080-11-3 (e-book)

Printed in the United States of America

To those who refuse to give up.

Richmond Swamps, October ACM 295

Gale force winds howled. Lightning flashed beyond cracks in the cellar door above us. Like a drum beat, the door banged violently against its latches, threatening to tear loose. Rain streamed through the edges of the frame into our small, earthen shelter. Already water was up to my knees and we were hanging from the steel frame that held up the ceiling.

Colleen clung to me in a death grip. My eleven-year-old sister had a bad case of the storm tremors that left her paralyzed in fear. I felt the urge, yet focused on her as I adjusted the harness that held us mostly above water.

"Don't let go, Regina," Colleen said through clattering teeth.

I gave her a squeeze. "It'll be okay, sis." *Hold on a little longer.*

Her head nodded acknowledgement, yet she trembled. Last year we'd found neighbors who had drowned in a similar cellar. Their pit had filled with rainwater. When they tried to escape, a tree that had fallen over the opening blocked them.

Colleen's breathing grew shallow. Her pulse raced. She had to be exhausted from shivering in the heat, though she hadn't whimpered. She didn't want me to feel sorry for

1

her. With each storm, she got worse. There was no getting used to them; no immunization eased the terror they brought. What kept me going was my need to protect my sister. I held her tight for me as much as for her.

Across the hollowed out pit we called a cellar, Mom flashed a light. She checked ropes securing what food and bedding we'd brought down. Water was above her waist and had soaked our supplies, yet the ropes held. She turned out the light plunging us back into darkness.

Waiting through the third hurricane of the season, I couldn't help wondering what it was like beyond the Great Barrier Wall and whether I might make it on the other side. That was if I survived this and found a way over the Wall. After all, the coastal swamps and scattered islands were the only home I'd known.

The World Federation had built the Wall to hold back rising seas from abrupt climate change. And to create a place outside the Federation to dump outcasts like my mom before Colleen and I were born. When I'd asked Mom about what happened, she refused to talk about the past. "Use your energy to stay alive and do your best," she'd said.

Lightning struck nearby. Wood splintered above us. The cellar door held, but I worried. I said a prayer for the storm to spare us and realized how pathetic I sounded. Praying to the Grand Old Dames who condemned us to this slice of drenched islands was a waste of energy better focused on survival.

The door banged in an unnerving rhythm, weakening the latches. Then as suddenly as the storm began, it simmered down. It didn't intend to kill us this time, merely to wear us down and test our resolve. Every act of survival was protest against what the Federation had done to us.

Winds ceased torturing the door, but calm was as unnerving as the storm. I held my breath, hoping this wasn't the eye of the hurricane with more to come. Rain slowed to a trickle and stopped. Our faded green canvas clothes were soaked and humidity wouldn't let us dry out, but I breathed easier.

Light poked through cracks in the cellar door above us, the first sign of hope in hours. The storm was ending. In a few months, winter, such as it was, would bring an end to these storms. It had in the past, though with temperatures rising, hurricane season kept growing longer and more intense.

"You okay, Mom?" I called out across the dark shadows.

"Never better," Mom said in a steady voice intended to calm Colleen. She turned on a flashlight so we could see. "Stake claim to our property."

The storm was bad enough, but scavengers were like Biblical locusts, swarming the land, stripping it bare, and taking what little survived.

I unstrapped myself from the harness anchored to rusted steel pipes that went some twenty feet into the ground below us. When I dropped, the water in the cellar was above my waist. I unfastened Colleen and eased her onto a nearby ledge. Three years younger, she was much shorter, and I didn't want her to panic.

She hugged me tight. "Thanks, Regina," she whispered.

The words carried dread that I might abandon her to the storm. *Never.*

Colleen let go and eased her way around the pit to Mom, who was inspecting our belongings. Mom gave her a quick hug and pushed her toward the cellar door. We had work to do.

"Come on, sis," I said after I unlatched the cellar door.

I pushed open the door, grabbed my crossbow, and pulled myself up to our wind-whipped world. The river channels frothed with tension. Tree limbs scattered around our small island: firewood for cooking. Our orange and apple trees had shed much of their fruit across the clearing. A hint of citrus filled the air as if the storm had swept away our usual dank swampy aromas.

"Gather what you can," I whispered and ran toward our water system.

The roof had blown off our water tanks and lay under fallen tree branches. The river-water tank was on its side with the lid missing. Water spilled onto the mud. A two-inch gash poked through the side of the tank. I wasn't sure if we could repair it and I couldn't see the lid.

Dreading the loss of clean water, I examined the fresh-water tank, which remained upright. The float showed three-quarters full, but the ground was so soaked, I couldn't be sure there wasn't a leak. At least I spotted no gaping holes and the lid protected the precious contents.

We would have to be water-frugal until Mom and I could fix the river-water tank and make sure the water purifiers worked.

Nearby, roof timbers had ripped off our cabin. The walls were battered yet our home stood. Checking the inside and the rest of our possessions would have to wait. We had to make sure scavengers knew we could get by.

While Colleen gathered fruit, I hurried down to our boat dock. I slung my crossbow over my shoulder so I could use both hands to steady myself down slippery rocks covered in topsoil the storm tried to wash away.

The water had risen five feet and broke in waves over our rocky shores. The river had swamped our docking cove. Thankfully, Mom and I had secured her skiff's mooring rope to trees on what had been dry ground. Now the boat was in the channel. Floating was good. Slow leaks we could fix, but a gash or shattered frame would doom us.

A power boat motored up the channel toward our island. Eyeing our skiff, scavengers in green-canvas rags looked for anything they could use. I grabbed our boat's nylon rope and hauled it in.

The scavengers drew closer. I wrapped the rope around my left arm, pulled my crossbow from my shoulder, and removed the safety. One of the scavengers was a girl a year older than me whom I'd bartered with on occasion. I aimed the bow. *Stay away.*

An older scavenger woman who didn't look to be the girl's mother waved in a friendly manner and motored closer. She scanned our island. "You survived?"

It sounded more like a question than a statement of fact. I had the impression she was disappointed. After all, wood and supplies were scarce on this side of the Wall.

I steadied my bow. "We have food, water, and the skiff," I said as proof that we could carry on. I had no doubt the woman would have taken those if I hadn't been there.

The motorboat moved away. "Good luck," the scavenger woman said. She didn't offer to help us rebuild.

A gun cocked behind me. I turned to see Mom atop a rocky ledge with Colleen at her side. She held her rifle aimed at the horizon. I followed her line of sight to a bounty boat across the channel. Two women in brown alligator leather used binoculars to scan us.

Bounty hunters were outcasts like us who picked up lost girls during and after storms. They made their living by selling their captives into slavery beyond the Wall to fill jobs Federation citizens didn't want like mine and farm laborers. I'd lost a friend last year when bounty hunters got to her before I could.

It had been that way all my life. Neighbors barely survived on shrinking islands, all due to crimes they or their ancestors may have committed in the misty past. *But why must the sins of the mothers fall upon their daughters?* After all, Colleen and I were born here.

The bounty hunters across the channel watched me reel in the nylon rope and tie our skiff to a sturdy tree. I was not about to let them take Colleen or me, despite the promise of shelter and meals beyond the Wall. I didn't trust their lies.

The Federation, and their police dogs, the Department of Antiquities, didn't want us outcasts to know that before they took over, the lands around Richmond had been fertile instead of swamps. Our dwindling island had once been the top of a tree-covered hill.

Over the past few centuries, abrupt climate change had altered so much, and it was the job of Antiquities agents to see that nothing from the past surfaced. Yet the sunken Richmond ruins all around us revealed secrets if we held on long enough and knew where to search.

Out in the channel, the bounty boat and the scavengers disappeared behind a nearby island to prey on other families. I worried about neighbors and friends, yet if I didn't help Mom, we wouldn't have a home.

As I secured our skiff, I spotted a leak that needed a weld. Still, a leaky skiff was better than none. Nearby was my log-boat, which I'd carved out of a fallen tree-trunk and made big enough for me and my sister. I'd left it strapped to a tree above the water. Satisfied that we had boats, I headed uphill.

While I thrived on learning about our forbidden past, I cursed my photographic memory, which made me a freak in a world forbidden to read books. This memory refused to let me forget illegal books I'd salvaged that told of the follies of the past. I couldn't fathom knowing how to prevent abrupt climate change and not acting. Yet that was my conclusion after reading books by Lamella Marshall, written in what she called the late twenty-first century, some three-hundred years ago. She'd written a complete history of her time, while climate ran amuck.

From the clearing atop our island, I scanned the channels on all sides. Another scavenger crew moved down river, to where storm surges would have been more devastating. Since we all lived off what we salvaged, it was hard to blame them, yet I did. *Salvage the depths. Don't steal from neighbors.*

I discovered our water-tank lid entangled in bushes. I pulled it free and rolled it toward the water system. While Colleen picked up fallen branches for firewood, I joined

Mom by the six-foot-tall aluminum river-water tank.

"We can fix it," she said, pointing to a gash in the seam.

I nodded and ran into our cabin. The kitchen table lay shattered in the corner, the wood in splinters. Bed frames remained nailed to the floor. We'd taken the rest of the bedding into the cellar, where it lay soaked. The wood-burning stove was on its side.

In the back of the cabin, I located a latched compartment beneath the floor from which I grabbed tubes of polymer paste we'd salvaged from the depths. Most of the paste had hardened, but if we cut into the tubes, some had malleable material to plug the water-tank hole. I grabbed two round aluminum strips and ran out to the water system.

Mom helped Colleen build a fire with damp wood in a wheeled barrow so they could move the fire under the tank. I climbed into the water container, cut polymer shavings over the gash, and scooped out a dollop of goo.

The fire had me feverish. Fumes from the polymer choked my throat as the material oozed into the seam. While Mom used tongs to place a circle of aluminum beneath the hole, I spread more material and moved away to keep my sweat from contaminating the weld.

When the polymer began to ooze from the heat, I applied a circle of aluminum above the opening, used my knife handle to press it down, and hoped it would hold. Then I climbed out and collapsed onto the wet grass.

While we waited for the seam to cool, we made repairs to the roof and walls of our cabin to provide shelter for the night. Then the three of us pushed the river-water tank upright and reattached the purifier's pipes.

Using a rusted bicycle frame, I pumped muddy water from the nearby channel into the tank. After the tank was half-full, and not leaking, I helped Mom reattach the tank's lid and make sure the burners would draw sterilized water into the fresh tank.

By the time we finished, I was exhausted, yet worried about my salvage partner. "I'm going to check on Magdalena."

"Not until we've finished repairs," Mom said. Her eyes narrowed. "Not with bounty hunters and scavengers out."

"I'll be extra careful," I said.

"Not now."

There was no arguing when Mom set her mind like this, but I couldn't focus. Magdalena lived in the outer channels, where storm surges were rougher.

She was the closest I had to a friend. I'd skipped two grades in the only remaining school the Federation hadn't closed, where Mom had bartered dearly for Colleen and me to attend. It was hard to make friends with older classmates or those my age in lower grades. Magdalena didn't mind. She was my age, a good diver, and helped me salvage from the drowned ruins of Richmond.

I wished we had those simple twenty-first century communicators. But finding working units was hard, and there were no towers or hubs in the swamps. Besides, Antiquities agents could track signals. For girls, the punishment for getting caught was slavery in the Federation as happened to one of our neighbors. For women, they offered slow execution as an example to others. One of the Federation's favorite sentences was the cage, submerged at high tide.

When I didn't move fast enough, Mom shook me. "No sulking. We need dry firewood. The skiff needs repairs. There's work to do. Get busy."

But I didn't want to lose another friend.

* * *

Colleen gathered anything that, if dry, would burn. She was a scurrying squirrel, afraid of being left behind like a neighbor up north. When they lost their fishing gear during a storm and couldn't gather enough food, they left their youngest daughter on a barren island for the bounty hunters.

Unburdened by knowledge of the past, surviving day-by-day was all that mattered to Colleen and our neighbors. The Federation had turned us into wild animals on the verge of extinction. *Not me.*

I was determined not only to survive, but to help neighbors be self-sufficient and independent of the Federation. Maybe someday, before the swamps disappeared altogether, we could make it over the Wall. Somehow all that ancient knowledge I'd gathered from illegal books had to figure in. But first, I needed my salvage partner.

Deep in the recesses of my gut I knew she needed help. Magdalena was an only child. Her mom often got depressed that their island was too small to survive on and that storms kept coming. With each passing day, my friend had to do more fishing, gardening, repairs, and cooking by herself. She had to take on her mom's role, and she was only fifteen.

While Mom made repairs inside the cabin and Colleen gathered wood on the other side of the island, I grabbed my log-boat and paddled out into the frothy channel. The current was strong, but heading my way, out toward the outer islands where Magdalena lived. My heart ached over what I might find.

My arms burned from holding Colleen during the storm and making repairs. I didn't want to defy Mom, who had provided me a home and sacrificed for schooling, but I had to know if my friend had survived.

I paddled hard across the channel and made my way around a nearby island. The Krause family was making sure scavengers knew they still claimed their island. Ms. Krause waved. I wasn't a scavenger risk with my small boat, so I waved back.

"Need any help?" I asked.

"We're fine. Watch for scavengers southeast of here. And bounty hunters."

"Thanks, ma'am."

Along the southeast side of Krause's island, I hid among cattails and sunken bushes. Thanks to binoculars and my memory, I confirmed that the bounty boat I'd seen before was the one now hovering in the distance. It had the same registration numbers on the bow. One bounty hunter stood at the bow using binoculars.

Next to her were two girls in chains. Their green-canvas clothes were tattered. Their faces looked more resigned than terrified. I recognized one from out Magdalena's way, a girl whose mom couldn't afford to barter for school. Maybe she would be better off in a Federation work camp, but even twenty-first century nations had abolished slavery.

Unable to think how to rescue the girls from armed bounty hunters, or how to feed them if I did, I headed north, paddling hard against the swift current dragging debris of people's lives. In a round-about way I made it to an island across from three scavenger boats. As I feared, they'd converged on Magdalena's home.

I didn't see her. I didn't see her cabin, either. Logs from her home scattered about the island and floated in the channel nearby. Two green-clad scavenger women dragged timbers toward the shore. A crew of three loaded the fresh-water tank onto their boat. Another carried the water purifiers. Two other scavenger boats waited in the channel for the first boats to get their fill and leave. Competition was fierce but they didn't want to lose their lives bickering over a rich find.

A gray Department of Antiquities boat motored past. They were the police, the authorities, but the agents made no attempt to stop the scavengers from stripping the island and Magdalena's family of what they needed to survive. They also didn't interfere with the nearby bounty hunters, since they delivered girls to be slaves.

With the current in my favor, I set out toward the side of Magdalena's island away from the scavengers. The bubbly channel was strong, shoving my log-boat out toward the open sea, a mile away. Despite aching muscles, I paddled hard across the current to reach quiet eddies on the southeast side of the island. Trees had uprooted from a storm surge. Bushes had pulled free. Logs floated in the water, banging against my boat. I pulled closer for a better look.

Magdalena huddled in a pool of water amidst rocks, her head bobbing. She didn't seem to notice me. I recognized the paralyzing storm tremors. When they caught hold, the mind shut down.

I paddled beside her. "Where's your mom?" I whispered.

Sweat made it hard to tell, but I gathered she'd been crying until her tears stopped. She pointed across the channel.

"She left?" I held her feverish hand, which trembled in mine.

Magdalena shrugged. "House gone. Water gone. Mom gone."

"Is she coming back?"

Eyes vacant, my friend shook her head.

"We have to claim your island."

Her words came out slowly. "I can't make it. Mom took the boat."

"Did she go for help?" I said as encouragement.

Magdalena looked up, her eyes those of an old woman. "Mom said wait for bounty hunters. They'll come after scavengers leave."

"No, Magdalena. Don't. You don't want slavery."

"No boat; no water; no home. I'm a burden with no hope."

"Stop it. You're my friend. We'll work this out. If you won't defend your home, then climb in."

She shook her head. "No use."

"Hurry," I said. "A bounty woman is coming." I pointed uphill.

A woman in a brown alligator outfit with binoculars

scanned the small island. She spotted us and hiked down the slope toward us.

Upon seeing the bounty hunter, Magdalena climbed in.

"Wait right there," the bounty woman said. She lifted a tranquilizer gun but lost her footing.

I placed my crossbow in my lap. I was tempted to shoot, but while Antiquities agents wouldn't stop bounty hunters and scavengers, they would hunt me down for shooting one.

Before the alligator woman raised her gun again, I paddled around bushes and cattails, staying out of the swift current until we were halfway back to the scavenger cove. The bounty hunter followed us partway but then hurried to the cove, where she'd left her boat.

"Paddle," I said to Magdalena. "The current is too strong to do this alone."

We pushed out into the main channel. Immediately the rush of water shoved us toward the sea. Branches and clothes rushed our way, threatening to entangle us. I aimed into the current to lower our profile and we paddled hard toward a nearby island. When I looked back, the bounty hunter boat moved away from the cove.

We paddled around the island, keeping to quieter waters and then pushed against the current to reach another island. We hid in the cattails, thankful for the smallness of my log-boat. Magdalena trembled, drawing into herself like a wounded mouse.

After the bounty boat passed, we crossed another channel and another. By the time we reached the Krause family island, the bounty boat had turned around and was scouring nearby islands more closely. We barely made it into the cattails before the boat began motoring around Krause Island. It was too late to try for my home island. Besides, I didn't want Mom turning Magdalena over to save Colleen and me.

Bounty hunter pay was high enough for them to keep hunting until they found us, and to make trouble for Mom if they didn't. With nowhere else to run, we climbed out of the log-boat and carried it up behind rocks.

From where we crouched, we watched the bounty boat with three green-clad girls chained to the bow railing. Two brown-clothed bounty hunters scanned us with binoculars. I hoped in the oppressive heat that they couldn't pick up our infrared signals. I pulled out my crossbow in case. I wouldn't go without a fight.

"Wouldn't it be better to let them take me?" Magdalena said. "I don't want to be a burden."

"Don't you dare," I said, huddling next to her. "Friends look out for each other."

"Even my mom didn't stick around."

"That doesn't mean you have to give up."

I knew it was hard, but hard didn't mean you surrendered. Magdalena squeezed my hand in a manner that got me worried she was saying goodbye.

"If they catch you, they catch me," I said before she did something rash.

She sighed. "You're the best friend in the world. Do you really think I have a chance?"

I didn't, though I wasn't ready to quit. "Together we'll search for your mom and a place for you to live."

"She's not coming back."

"Why? What happened?"

* * *

Magdalena shrugged and watched the bounty hunters circle the island. She leaned closer and whispered. "The wind tore the door off the cellar. Mom had a ratty old doll from her mom. The wind took the doll. In the middle of the storm, Mom ran out to find it. I couldn't stop her from rowing away. A big wave destroyed the boat. I'm sure she drowned. All for a stupid doll." Despite the turmoil in her face, she shed no more tears.

I was in shock. I felt attachments to books I'd read, but I couldn't imagine going into a storm to protect them. Life was too precious, even in the swamps.

After the bounty boat circled the island the third time, it crossed to Mom's island. She stood on a ledge, her rifle pointed out. I couldn't hear what they said, but the bounty boat moved on. I aimed my bow in case they returned.

"We have no surplus," a woman's voice said from behind us.

I turned to face the barrel of Ms. Krause's shotgun.

"We're leaving, ma'am," I said. "Just avoiding bounty hunters."

Her face softened. "Sorry. I don't know which is worse, the storms or the scum who thrive on suffering."

"Thanks for your hospitality, ma'am." I dragged my boat toward the shore.

Magdalena helped me put the log-boat into the water. We checked one last time for the bounty boat and paddled against the current into Mom's cove.

Gun at her side, she greeted us by her skiff. "You abandoned your chores."

"I'm sorry, Mom. Magdalena needed help. She lost her mom and her home. Scavengers cleaned the place. Then bounty hunters came."

"So that's why they were here." Holding onto a tree trunk, Mom moved along a rocky ledge. Then she turned to Magdalena. "I'm very sorry for your loss. We don't have much and Regina should be helping to fix things."

"I'm sorry, ma'am," Magdalena said. "I should have let the bounty woman take me."

"No, Mom. We can't. She's my best friend. We have to help. At least until we find her a home."

Mom sighed. "You'll have to scrounge extra food. We lost fruit and fish are scarce."

"I understand, Mom."

"Do you?"

"I won't abandon my friend. We'll just have to salvage the depths."

"Antiquities patrols are making that impossible. They don't want us disturbing cultural artifacts they deny exist."

Mom turned to Magdalena. "If you help make repairs, you can stay the night."

"Thanks, ma'am." Magdalena forced a smile. "How can I help?"

* * *

After Magdalena helped us tar the roof and walls, I led her down to my log-boat.

Colleen joined us. "Can I come?"

"Mom needs you to look after her," I said. Colleen wasn't buying it so I added, "We have little room for salvage as it is."

"Mom will make me do your chores."

"I'll make it up to you. We need to find something so Magdalena has a home."

Colleen sulked on the ledge above the cove. I disassembled my crossbow, wrapped it in plastic, and stored it in a compartment in the back of my boat. Then I dug up a corroded aluminum funnel with a sealed opening. I placed the funnel in the middle of the log and paddled away from shore.

"What do we need that for?" Despite the spark of curiosity, Magdalena's eyes drooped, showing the full weight of losing her mom and home.

I paddled us out into the channel, and let the current carry us east. "The funnel is great for catching rain water."

She drew her arms in tight to her chest: storm tremors.

"No more storms today," I said, feeling terrible for scaring her. I was asking too much to ask her to dive after losing her mom and home, but I needed help. Besides, we were doing this for her.

Tears streamed down her cheeks. "I don't know what would have happened to me if you hadn't come."

"That's what friends do," I said, paddling us northward.

She shrugged. "I know you want to help, but do we have to dive?"

"We find the best salvage after a storm stirs up

15

sediment. Maybe it exposed something we can barter."

I wanted to rip the resignation from Magdalena before it got both of us killed. This wasn't her first loss. She and her mom had been unable to save her sister five years ago during another storm. It was hard not to resign when each year the seas swallowed more of your life. Becoming a Federation slave sounded reassuring, except I'd heard rumors of girls dying in the mines and factories and being worked to death on the farms.

We approached the waters over what had been a Richmond suburb. Scavengers had picked islands out here clean of human habitation and trees. Denuded islands offered no resistance to storms or sea. Only swamp grasses thrived.

We headed across a wider channel between smaller islands. A bounty boat motored across the horizon. I saw in Magdalena's eyes a yearning to be taken care of, a desire for shelter with food.

I pulled into the cover of cattails. "That's no life for you," I whispered as if the bounty hunter could hear this far.

"I don't want your mom mad at you and ..."

"She won't abandon me on account of you."

Magdalena picked up her paddle. "I won't let them catch you."

I was thankful she'd found something to keep her from giving up. I glanced at the cloudless sky. The sun blazed down on us like a fire—well it was.

While we waited for the bounty boat to pass, a gray Antiquities boat rounded a nearby island. Two girls stood chained to the bow rail. I recognized them from the school Magdalena and I went to. Antiquities agents scanned our island with binoculars and motored off. If it hadn't been for my spotting the bounty boat, the Antiquities agents might have caught us. I couldn't leave Colleen like that.

After the Antiquities boat was gone, we circled the

barren island to make sure no one else was there. Then we headed across water above a satellite community outside of Richmond.

We reached a small, treeless island. Waves broke in the distance where the sea fought the river current. Fishing was good out here though scavengers could grab you. One time I'd dangled my catch below the boat to keep it from scavengers, but hungry predators ate my fish. There was nothing more discouraging than getting home to find you had nothing left.

We hid the log-boat amidst cattails. Then I pulled four breathing bladders from a compartment of my boat. They weren't as good as scuba tanks, but those were luxuries reserved for bounty hunters and Antiquities patrols. "Are you up for this?"

Magdalena nodded though her heart wasn't into it.

"Do this for me," I said, filling my breathing bladders. "I don't want to lose my only friend."

She laughed until tears streamed down her cheeks. "You're the only friend who came to check on me."

"Then it's settled. We do this for each other." I clasped her arm. "Blood sisters."

Magdalena nodded with enthusiasm and made sure Colleen's breathing bladders were full.

I attached mine to a belt holding up my canvas shorts, removed my green canvas top, and slid into the water. Then I pulled goggles over my eyes. I checked the knife on my belt and ducked under water to make sure there were no gators or other predators lurking nearby.

When I surfaced, Magdalena was ready to dive. She managed a smile. "Thanks. I won't let you down."

The sun in the western sky cast no shadows onto this side of the island. I pointed westward. "The dive site is a thousand feet out and straight down. Don't use breathing bladders until we dive. It's a hundred feet down. Don't take any chances." I didn't remind her of the bends. I didn't need to give her something else to worry about. Besides, if it came to that, the bends would be the least of her troubles.

* * *

When we reached the spot I picked to dive, I double-checked the position of the sun and the island.

"This is it," I said.

"Let's do it," Magdalena said without conviction.

We attached breathing bladders and descended into the cloudy depths. Sediment was shifting in the strong channel current, making it as dark as the storm at night.

I held off using my only flashlight so we didn't trigger Antiquities sensors. Magdalena swam close, bumping into me to get her bearings. Before we touched bottom, I turned on the light for a quick look.

Below was an Antiquities mine in the shape of a crab. It hadn't been there during my last visit, which meant they'd found this spot and were interested.

Magdalena pointed to the mine and then up. I pointed across a plateau toward a stone house I'd visited once before. The roof and shingles were gone, probably wood frame and fiberglass, judging by scraps I'd found. The doors and windows were gone. Yet the walls stood guard like a medieval castle, resisting the ravages of time—I'd read too many history texts.

I took a good look, turned out the light, and swam closer.

From my last visit, I knew the drywall had turned to mush. The wood furniture had rotted, though varnish remained as a ghost of what lay beneath. Metal cabinets and appliances had corroded to uselessness. I'd salvaged the stainless cook-wear and bartered for a goat to provide my sister milk. She owed her good bones and teeth to that goat.

The homeowners had been well off, with nice things even by twenty-first century references. They'd been frugal, using solar panels that lay corroded and in pieces behind the house. A wind generator had collapsed nearby. I'd hoped to salvage something off it, but from the look of nearby debris, someone had already stripped the site. I also expected to find something of use in the home's basement, which I hadn't had time to explore before.

On my prior visit, I'd cursed how these well-meaning souls had protected their precious books and electronics in biodegradable plastic. Maybe they didn't know. The paper had turned to mush, the memory devices had given up their memories, and the electronics had corroded beyond repair.

How did I know they'd used biodegradable plastics? Sometimes the plastic seams or seals survived, looking similar to their less biodegradable cousins. These folk had been good for the ecology but bad at preservation. The only surviving evidence that they had books—a title on leather with no book pages behind—was volume one of Lamella Marshall's *History of the Twenty-first Century*.

As Magdalena and I approached the house, I flipped on the light.

Since my last visit, Antiquities had strung wire across all the openings on the first and second floor. There would be sensors if we got any closer and trip wires intended to cause injury or warn us away. Beyond the deterrent, Antiquities had made no attempt to preserve anything. Why would they? The only past they preserved began with the Federation.

I swam up over the house and studied the shell of the structure. Wires, various shapes of mines, and traps covered the open roof gap like a spider's web. There was no going in. If we survived whatever blasts they might trigger, we would be out of oxygen long before Antiquities patrols came for us. The site had been worth a look, but we would have to scrounge harder for a way to help my friend.

Motioning for Magdalena to follow, I turned off the light and swam toward the island. I recalled texts mentioning how cautious people had become before the Federation. This stone house overlooked a now sunken valley a hundred feet below. There could be more sites down there, but they were too deep to dive with breathing bladders. Only Antiquities agents and a few bounty hunters had deep salvage tanks.

In the shimmer of light from the surface above, something caught my eye. It wouldn't have been visible from the stone house even before the deluge. Yet it held possibilities, if for no other reason than it was higher than the house, a safe haven from earlier floods.

As I swam closer, a cave opening appeared. Magdalena tugged my arm to swim uphill to the island. I shook my head. Then she pulled me toward the cave.

Under water, you had to trust your partner, so I followed her into the cave before looking back. Three points of light moved in the distance. Antiquities divers with tanks.

If Antiquities caught us out here, they would use starvation, torture, and submerged cages until we told everything we knew about underwater treasures. Or so I'd heard. No one ever returned from interrogation. If they were lucky, or unlucky, they became Federation slaves.

The outside lights moved toward the stone building below us. When they were gone, I flashed my light to take in as wide an image of the cave as I could like a camera. In the ensuing darkness, Magdalena squeezed my arm. I sensed her terror, but forced myself to concentrate on the image I'd seen, committing it to memory. The cave was shallow, natural as in not made by humans. It might have provided short-term shelter from past storms until it flooded. I imagined a campfire, though evidence would have washed away long ago. Aside from providing shelter from Antiquities agents, this was disheartening. There was no salvage potential.

Magdalena brought my hand to her breathing bladder; she was worried. She pulled me toward the cave opening to leave. Outside, the three lights moved closer. In the muddy water I could just make out the gray wetsuits worn by Antiquities divers. I couldn't let them catch my friend and give her the worst slave job they could think of. Environmental-hazard cleanup came to mind.

I pulled her deeper into the cave. We couldn't risk my light to hunt for another way out. Instead, I stood where I'd gotten my image, closed my eyes, and studied it again. There were no breaks in the wall before me. My hands and foot found no openings behind. Then I looked up at my remembered picture.

Barely visible at the top of the frame was an opening, a possible tunnel that would have been useless when this was dry. The ceiling above the cave and into the tunnel were black, charred blacker than the rest of the cave. Either that or it was a darker shade of rock.

I switched breathing bladders, directed Magdalena's hands to do the same, and swam up to the opening in the ceiling. It was just big enough for us to swim through if we tucked the breathing bladder around our necks. I tugged Magdalena up, let her feel the gap, and entered into darkness that let me realize how much Antiquities light was entering the cave. By feel I made my way up, horizontal, and up some more, haunted by the nagging fear that this was a dead-end or worse, a trap.

The tunnel curved and grew narrower until I could barely squeeze through. Then it widened. Unable to feel the depth of space around me, I flipped on the flashlight. Magdalena swam up behind and glanced around in amazement. We were in a chamber, a room carved by human hands. There was a path from where we entered to a full sized door. Lining the walls around us were plastic shelves holding stacks of plastic packages, and not the biodegradable variety.

Magdalena pointed to her breathing bladder and to the space we'd left. I shook my head and gave her the Antiquities signal. *What if they're following us?* After all, they had much better diving equipment.

We needed to keep moving, but I was drawn to a richer discovery than any I'd uncovered so far, one that could secure a home for my friend.

Nearby was the six volume set from Lamella Marshall, well preserved. I held the volumes with reverence, unwilling to let Antiquities destroy these as they had so many others. There had to be hundreds or thousands of physical print books. My breath caught.

There were too many books and they weighted too much to carry with us. Besides, we were running out of oxygen and we didn't know how to reach the surface.

Nearby was an old Franklin stove, protected in plastic. Magdalena pointed to a stack of pots, dishes, silver, and home-building tools. That was what we needed. But books nourished the soul. *Well, not if we didn't survive.*

There was no way back: we didn't have enough oxygen and Antiquities agents were waiting. We had to find a way forward and a way to stop agents from following. We dragged the Franklin stove to the tunnel leading down, pushed the top into the hole, and shoved it down as far as we could. Then we wedged tools into gaps between the stove and the tunnel walls to slow them down.

I pocketed a plastic-wrapped memory chip I hoped held some of the written treasures. Maybe a well-preserved computer device that I'd rebuilt would reveal its secrets. I tried the door at the other end of the watery room. It refused to budge.

Magdalena's face took on the cast of storm terrors. I had to act before she panicked. Recalling twenty-first century how-to texts, I examined the door. The hinges were on our side. Using screwdrivers and pliers from among the tools, we removed the hinge post and pulled the door open.

Beyond was another flooded room with stairs that led up. Though there was no human dwelling on the surface, up was our best option.

We carried pans, silverware, and tools in their plastic containers into the next room and up the stairs. I figured we'd descended a hundred-twenty feet and risen eighty. We were close, though you could drown in an inch of water.

The stairs led past rooms with beds and shreds of clothes that had not survived the flood. If this had been the owner's shelter during the early years, I hoped they'd made it to higher ground. As we swam and walked up, I looked for exits. Then we hit a dead-end. The framed drywall ceiling had disintegrated, leaving stone above us.

Magdalena was gulping air, ready to panic. She offered me what she had left. I refused. I'd gotten her into this. I couldn't live with her death.

The owners would have needed a way to get fresh air and to exhaust cooking fumes from the kitchen below us. I led Magdalena above the kitchen to a large-diameter pipe. We used metal cutters, pliers, and a screwdriver to pry the aluminum open. Then we climbed into the enclosure. I turned out the light and followed the path up.

After ten feet, I tumbled out into the channel. Lights moved below us: a submarine, one of Antiquities' small drone-probes. Above was daylight. I helped Magdalena out of the tunnel and pushed her toward the island.

Tugging our treasure behind us, we kicked our way up the side of the underwater hill to the surface. We came up among cattails and sucked in fresh air. Magdalena was gasping. I pushed her to shore and dragged our treasure onto the rocks.

"That was close," she said.

I nodded. "You okay?"

She took a long breath and leaned back to take in the sky. She looked more alive than at any time since I'd found her. Trembling, she hugged me. The terror of what had almost happened seeped into my thoughts. We weren't out of this yet.

A gray Antiquities boat remained in the channel

between us and home. Leaving our salvage on shore, we swam to the log-boat. I armed my crossbow and peered out through the cattails. Using binoculars I spotted the captain with a handheld device.

The sun would set soon, giving us the cover of night, but with temperatures dropping, our infrared images would show up on their scanners.

While we waited, we returned with the log-boat to our treasure and nibbled on cattails for nourishment. Then we fastened our salvage goods to the funnel and that to a hook beneath the log-boat. The funnel tip would reduce drag while we paddled up the channel.

Magdalena refilled the breathing bladders. "What if they catch us?"

"We dump the goods, dive, and hide."

She looked dubious but forced a smile.

As the sun set, the captain and a sailor changed into diving gear. They took extra scuba tanks and descended using a mini-sub to pull them to the depths. I didn't see anyone else on the patrol boat. They must have dropped off any girls they'd captured.

"We have to chance it," I said.

I handed her a paddle and aimed us across the swift flow of the channel, diagonally past the Antiquities boat. Struggling against the current would leave us exposed for a long time. Then I had a better idea.

We pulled up behind the patrol boat, where they kept a motorized dingy and tied our mooring rope. Magdalena looked ready to strangle me as I unlatched the tiny craft and attached it to the log-boat. After releasing the rope, we paddled away from the patrol.

When we were far enough out of earshot, I started the motor and used the dingy to pull us upstream. After we reached the channel north of my home, we cast the dingy adrift and paddled into Mom's cove. As much as we could have used the speed-boat, it had tracking chips.

* * *

As night settled in, Mom greeted us by her skiff. In the moonlight, Colleen stood on the ledge above scanning the horizon with binoculars.

"You had me worried sick," Mom said.

"We found something," I said.

"It doesn't matter if you don't live to enjoy it." Mom moved closer. "Show me your find."

Magdalena and I dragged the funnel and attached bundle from beneath my boat and handed items up to Mom.

She stacked them on a rocky ledge, helped us out, and gave us both a hug. "You did well. This will buy a good start for your friend. But you can't keep taking risks. I thought bounty hunters or Antiquities had grabbed you."

"They almost did, Mom. But Magdalena helped by watching my back. She's a great partner."

Magdalena looked puzzled. Then she squeezed my hand. "Friends watch out for each other."

I squeezed back.

Colleen clung to my other arm and stared up at me. A touch of her night terrors crossed her face and faded away. I kissed her forehead.

In the weeks that followed, rumors floated through the Richmond Swamps. Antiquities agents were hopping mad. Responding to tripped sensors around a forbidden site, two of their divers pursued a couple salvagers. Convinced they'd cornered the scoundrels, the divers removed their tanks to enter a narrow tunnel. A Franklin stove blocked their way. They ran out of oxygen before they could back out of the tunnel to reach their tanks and before a rescue crew could help them.

The treasure room might still be there when I returned. But in the meantime, Magdalena could stay with us until we found her a new home.

BOOKS BY LANCE ERLICK

REGINA SHEN: RESILIENCE (Regina Shen book 1)

Outcast Regina Shen is forced by the World Federation to live on the seaward side of barrier walls built to hold back rising seas from abrupt climate change. A hurricane threatens to destroy what's left of her world, tearing Regina from her family.

Global fertility has collapsed. Chief Inspector Joanne Demarco of the notorious Department of Antiquities believes Regina holds the key to avoid extinction. Regina fights to stay alive and avoid capture while hunting for her family. Does she have the resilience to survive?

REGINA SHEN: VIGILANCE (Regina Shen book 2)

Regina Shen is pursued by the notorious Department of Antiquities for her unique DNA. She jumps the Barrier Wall into the Federation to find her kidnapped sister. Stuck on a heavily-guarded closed-university campus in the mountains, she must use her wits to escape and rescue her sister without letting either of two rival Antiquities inspectors capture her.

REGINA SHEN: DEFIANCE (Regina Shen book 3)

Rival Federation agents fight over capturing Regina to gain power amidst turmoil over who will become the new World Premier. Regina has to flee from Virginia through desert and wilderness to Alaska to hunt a treasure big enough to barter for her freedom and that of her sister.

THE REBEL WITHIN (Rebel Series book 1)

Annabelle Scott lives under the iron rule of a female-dominated régime that forces males to fight to the death to train the military elite. When pressed into service as a mechanized warrior to capture escaped boys, Annabelle stays true to herself by helping some escape. Her defiance endangers everyone she loves and thrusts her to a place of impossible life and death decisions.

THE REBEL TRAP (Rebel Series book 2)

Despite being a military recruit, Annabelle Scott rebels against her female-dominated régime by refusing to kill a handsome boy she fancies and helping him escape. Auditory implants and cameras allow her commander to watch her 24-7. Can she help the boy free his brother from a heavily-guarded geek institute without destroying her family or getting killed?

REBELS DIVIDED (Rebel Series book 3)

The first time Geo sees Annabelle, they meet as enemies and she doesn't kill him, which mystifies them both. It's after the 2nd Civil War with the nation divided into an all-female Federal Union and a warlord controlled Outland. The Outland warlord kidnaps Annabelle's sister and kills Geo's pa. Can Annabelle and Geo overcome mutual distrust and work together to rescue her sister and gain justice for his pa's murder? And will their feelings for each other derail or further their goals?

MAIDEN VOYAGE (short story)

Security Chief Nina Rekovic keeps the peace on the all-female Maiden's Ark that left Earth five years before. Distress signal says Earth is lost, stranding lunar colonists. Someone sabotages the vital fertility lab. While balancing Returners she sympathizes with, a dictatorial captain, and an estranged lover who betrays her, can Rekovic solve the conspiracy before she's imprisoned or worse?

WATCHING YOU (short story)

At the intersection of pervasive networks and the Patriot Act, we have the ability and some say the obligation to know everything about everyone. Can privacy survive? Can the individual endure?

Harold is a second-class citizen and a low-level worker in a government surveillance system charged with reviewing "criminal activity." He has private thoughts about a woman he's forbidden from approaching. He will not be deterred.

SHE-DEVIL ROCKS (novelette)

Inspired by *Lord of the Flies*.

Bullied as the smallest of thirteen boys in his class, Bradley is on a plane that crashes on a remote island with a bully who is out of control. Bradley meets a mysterious tomboy who shouldn't be there and has to learn to survive on the hostile island, deal with her, and come to terms with the bully.

ABOUT THE AUTHOR

Lance Erlick likes to explore the mysteries of intriguing worlds with interesting, often strong female guides facing and overcoming adversity as they try to change their world. He hopes readers will enjoy his writing as they discover different worlds, going places they may never have been.

He writes science fiction thrillers, appealing to young adult and adult readers. He is the author of *The Rebel Within, The Rebel Trap,* and *Rebels Divided,* three books in the Rebel series. In those stories, he explores the consequences of following conscience for those coming of age. He authored the Regina Shen series—*Regina Shen: Resilience, Regina Shen: Vigilance,* and *Regina Shen: Defiance.* This series takes place after abrupt climate change leads to the Great Collapse and a new society under the World Federation. A related short story is: *Regina Shen: Into the Storm.* Lance is also the author of unrelated short stories: *Maiden Voyage* and *Watching You.*

Find out more about the author and his work at LanceErlick.com. Go to that website to sign up to receive occasional email newsletters with links to free short stories, and updates on new releases and other writing developments.